I made this book out of memories from time I spent with my grandma.
Drawing some scenes made me cry and others made me laugh out loud.
It brings me so much joy to introduce you here to Muyeon Park,
my grandma, whom I call *Halmoni* in Korean. She devoted herself
to our family for a lifetime.

I love you, Halmoni.
—*Gee-eun Lee*

박무연
Muyeon Park

"Mommy, don't go!"

"Dear me, your mom will have to take a boat to work
to get across all these tears."

Grandma breaks a sweat again today as she tries to calm Gee-eun down.

"How about we make some delicious *kalguksu*?"
Grandma asks.

"Okay," Gee-eun answers.
"I can knead a little bit, too, Halmoni."

Grandma tugs off a piece of noodle dough, and
Gee-eun presses and shapes it with her small hands.

"Halmoni, can you guess what this is?"

"Is it a bear?"

"Nope! It's Mari, our fluffy Mari.
And this is Mom, and that's Dad.
And you and me are right here."

"Would you look at that?
Our Gee-eun is so good
with her hands."

Grandma slides shredded zucchini and clams in their shells
that go *tak tak tak* into the big pot of stock.
After that, she swishes in the white noodle strands,
and the kalguksu boils and bubbles.

**"Look at this, Halmoni.
Our whole family is in that bowl."**

"Oh yes, there we all are.
You tell them to hang on tight
to the noodles so they
stay afloat."

Grandma blows on a noodle for Gee-eun,
who sucks it in with one slurp
of her little mouth.

All full of kalguksu, Grandma's tummy puffs out like a balloon.
Gurgle, slosh, slosh. Gurgle, gurgle, slosh.

"Halmoni, I can hear water. The sound is coming from inside your tummy."

"Well, that's no surprise. There's a stream in there—and a forest too."

"Really? Is there? And what else?"

"A teeny tiny house that's warm and cozy, where your mom used to live."

"But Mommy's bigger than you!"

"Back then, she was even smaller
than you are now."

When Family Sports Day—which Gee-eun was waiting for
with such anticipation—finally arrives, she is not happy at all.

"It's not fair! Mom promised she would go with me this year.
We have to do the cheer dance
and the tug-of-war
and the running race together. . . .

Who can I go with now?"

"There, there, Gee-eun. You've got me.
They used to call me the Ox when I was young. **The Ox!**
I could pull all the other kids over with only one arm!

"I was the best at running too.
They called me Speedy Horse because I ran so fast."

"Wow! Really?"

"And when it comes to dancing—well, that goes without saying.
I just do my thing like this and like that.
It'll be a long time before your mom can keep up with me."

"You're the best, Halmoni!"

Gee-eun and Halmoni arrive on Family Sports Day to find
that Sohui and Dongjin are here with their moms, and Gangwoo
from the class across the hall even brought his dad too.
But Gee-eun is feeling confident. She has her grandma, after all.

Unfortunately, Gee-eun's team loses the tug-of-war.
But it doesn't matter, because there's still the running race.

Gee-eun and Grandma take their places.

"Ready, set . . ."

Gee-eun's heart goes *thump, thump, thump.*

"Go!"

All the pairs set off.

Gyungho and his mom are out in first place.

Before long, Wonhui and her mom and Sungyon and her mom
overtake Gee-eun and Halmoni.

Seonhee is running with her grandma too—
but they're running much faster.

"Halmoni, run!"

"All right!"

"Halmoni, fast!

Faster!

Even Faster!"

That's when it happens: Grandma trips and takes a tumble.

"But, Halmoni, you said . . .
you said you could run fast."

Gee-eun bursts into tears.

Gee-eun doesn't say a word on the walk home.

"Tell you what, Gee-eun. Shall we have a fried curry bun at the market?"

"Don't want to."

"Oh, let's have one on our way back—just one," Grandma says.

"I guess it's because I'm old . . ." Grandma speaks into her fresh curry bun. "I'm no good at running anymore."

"Halmoni, can't you become young again?"

"That's a thought. Shall I try?"

"Can I have one more, Halmoni?"

"It's going to be dinnertime soon . . ."

"Just one."

"All right then, but the second one will have to be our secret."

"Yep, our secret."

No matter how you may be feeling, curry buns are always delicious, especially when shared with Grandma.

"Let's get a mackerel to take home and grill for your dad."

"Get the biggest one! One as big as Dad.

Halmoni, who would win if Dad and a mackerel had a swimming race?"

"Your dad would be much faster, no question."

"Wow."

"We'd better get a pound of bean sprouts
to season the way your mom likes."

"I like bean sprouts too. Halmoni, have you
ever seen a bean sprout as big as me?"

"Oh yes. Just once. And I seasoned it and gave it to your mom."

"Next time you see one like that, season it for me. **Me!**"

"Of course. It'll be for my Gee-eun."

"Let's get a dozen eggs and fry some the way Gee-eun likes them," Grandma suggests.

"Make your favorite fluffy steamed egg too."

"Oh my, you're always looking out for me, Gee-eun."

"Halmoni, does the hen miss her eggs?"

"Of course. She surely does."

"Halmoni, when will Mom get home?"

"Once the mackerel is grilled all brown and crispy,
and the bean sprouts are smushed and softened with sesame oil,
and the eggs are fried up all yummy,
then she'll be here in no time."

Ding-dong, ding-dong!

"It's Mom and Dad!"

Gee-eun leaps up to get the door.

"You've all had a busy day today," Grandma calls from the kitchen.
"Hurry in here. Let's eat."

And they do!
Nothing beats a meal made by Grandma.

Today I went to Sports Day with Halmoni.
Halmoni fell over.
I should rub on some medicine for her.
Halmoni, let's have curry buns again soon.

Text and illustrations copyright © 2016 by Gee-eun Lee
Translation copyright © 2022 by Sophie Bowman

Previously published as *Halmeoni eomma* by WOONGJIN THINKBIG CO. LTD in South Korea in 2016. English translation rights arranged through S.B. Rights Agency–Stephanie Barrouillet on behalf of Woongjin Thinkbig Co., Ltd. Translated from Korean by Sophie Bowman. First published in English by Amazon Crossing Kids in collaboration with Amazon Crossing in 2022.

Published by Amazon Crossing Kids, New York, in collaboration with Amazon Crossing
www.apub.com

Amazon, Amazon Crossing, and all related logos are trademarks of Amazon.com, Inc., or its affiliates.

ISBN-13: 9781662508257 (hardcover)
ISBN-10: 1662508255 (hardcover)

The illustrations were rendered in colored pencil and paint.
Book design by Tanya Ross Hughes

Printed in China
First Edition
10 9 8 7 6 5 4 3 2 1